21st Century Junior Library

Growing New Plants

by Jennifer Colby

CHERRY LAKE PUBLISHING * ANN ARBOR, MICHIGAN

CHERRY LAKE
Publishing

Published in the United States of America by Cherry Lake Publishing
Ann Arbor, Michigan
www.cherrylakepublishing.com

Consultants: Elizabeth A. Glynn, Youth Education Coordinator, Matthaei Botanical
Gardens and Nichols Arboretum, University of Michigan; Marla Conn, ReadAbility, Inc.

Photo Credits: © DementevaJulia/Shutterstock Images, Cover, 14, 20; © Katrina Leigh/Shutterstock
Images, 4; © Alexander Raths/Thinkstock, 6; © WathanyuSowong/Shutterstock Images, 8;
© daniaphoto/Shutterstock Images, 10; © Africa Studio/Shutterstock Images, 12;
© Alexey U/Shutterstock Images, 16; © Stephanie Frey/Shutterstock Images, 18

LIBRARY OF CONGRESS CATALOGING-IN-PUBLICATION DATA
Colby, Jennifer, 1971-
  Growing new plants/by Jennifer Colby. – [Revised edition]
     pages cm.—(21st century junior library)
  Includes bibliographical references and index.
  ISBN 978-1-63188-036-0 (hardcover)—ISBN 978-1-63188-122-0 (pdf)—
ISBN 978-1-63188-079-7 (pbk.)—ISBN 978-1-63188-165-7 (ebook)
  1. Plant propagation–Juvenile literature. 2. Plants–Juvenile literature.
3. Gardening–Juvenile literature. I. Title. II. Series: 21st century junior library.
  SB406.7.C65 2014
  631.5'3–dc23   2014006281

*Cherry Lake Publishing would like to acknowledge the work of
The Partnership for 21st Century Skills.
Please visit* www.p21.org *for more information.*

Printed in the United States of America

CONTENTS

The roots of a plant grow down into the dirt.

Same or Different?

All plants have many things in common. They all need sunlight, air, and water. Their roots need room to grow.

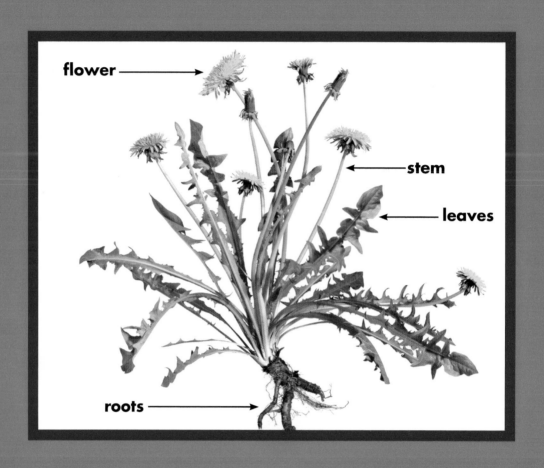

flower

stem

leaves

roots

All the parts of a plant work together to grow.

Roots take in **minerals** and water for the plant. The plant stem carries the water to all parts of the plant. Leaves use sunlight, air, and water to make food for the plant.

There are different kinds of plants. Some plants look dead in the winter. But they grow again in the spring. These plants are called **perennials**. Other plants grow from a seed, make seeds, and die in one year. These plants are called **annuals**.

Cosmos are annuals. They grow from
a seed and die in one year.

Plants grow new plants in many ways. Let's take a closer look at where new plants come from.

Create!

Have an adult help you find pictures of plants in magazines. Tape the pictures to a large piece of cardboard. Are the plants perennials or annuals? Ask an adult to help you find the answers. Then label your pictures.

The flowers of many plants grow fruit. Seeds grow inside the fruit. Do you see the seeds inside this apple?

Ways to Grow

Plants create new plants. This is called **reproduction**. How do plants do this? They create new plants in many ways.

Some plants create new plants by making seeds. They grow flowers that make new seeds. A seed can be planted in the dirt. With enough water and sunlight, the seed will grow into a new plant.

A bulb looks a little bit like an onion.

Some plants do not grow flowers. They make tiny **spores** instead of seeds. New plants grow from the spores. A fern is a kind of plant that grows from spores.

Some plants grow from **bulbs**. A tulip is a kind of plant that grows from bulbs. A bulb is made of many leaves. A tiny plant is inside the bulb. The bulb contains the food that the plant needs to grow.

Cuttings from a plant can grow in water or in dirt.

Some plants grow from **cuttings**.
A cutting is a small piece of a stem or
a leaf. The cutting will grow roots.

A cutting from a tree can be wrapped
into a cut on the stem of an older tree.
The cutting and the tree grow together to
become one plant. This is called **grafting**.

Make a Guess!

Ask a friend to name a plant. Guess if the plant grows
from seeds, spores, or bulbs. Try again! Were your
guesses right? Look in books or go online with an
adult to find out.

Dandelion seeds blow in the wind.

Plants on the Go

What do wind, water, people, birds, and insects have in common? They move parts of plants from one place to another. And they don't even know it! When they do this, they help new plants grow!

Wind and water move plant parts. A strong wind can carry seeds for many miles. Rain can wash seeds down hills and mountains.

Gardeners move plants from one place to another.

Sometimes people move plants. Gardeners divide a clump of roots in half. They replant each half to make two plants grow. People can take plant cuttings or plant seeds to grow new plants.

Birds and insects move **pollen** from one flower to another. The tiny pollen grains help the flower make seeds.

A new plant is growing from a seed.

Go outside and look at the plants around you. These plants came from seeds, spores, bulbs, cuttings, or roots.

Why not plant a seed? Then you can grow a new plant of your own!

Ask Questions!

Go to a garden center and ask the gardener how they grow plants. Find out which plants grow from seeds, spores, bulbs, cuttings, and roots.

GLOSSARY

annuals (AN-you-uhlz) plants that grow, flower, make seeds, and die in one year

bulbs (BUHLBZ) small, hard plant buds that grow underground and contain the food the plant needs to grow

cuttings (KUT-ingz) small pieces of a plant leaf or stem that can be used to grow a new plant

grafting (GRAF-ting) joining a piece of one plant onto another so they grow into one plant

minerals (MIN-ur-uhlz) substances found in nature that aren't alive but are needed in small amounts by many living things

perennials (purr-EN-ee-uhlz) plants that live for many years and flower many times

pollen (POL-uhn) dust-size grains that help make seeds in flowers

reproduction (ree-pruh-DUK-shuhn) the act of producing new plants or animals like their parents

spores (SPORZ) tiny parts of some plants that can grow into a new plant

FIND OUT MORE

BOOKS

Aston, Dianna, and Sylvia Long. *A Seed Is Sleepy*. Mankato, MN: Amicus, 2014.

Stewart, Melissa, and Carol Schwartz. *How Does a Seed Sprout? And Other Questions About Plants*. New York: Sterling Children's Books, 2014.

WEB SITES

National Geographic Kids—Planting Seeds
http://kids.nationalgeographic. com/kids/littlekids/science-experiments/plant-seeds
Step-by-step instructions on how to grow your own plant from a seed.

University of Illinois Extension—The Great Plant Escape: Is It Dust, Dirt, Dandruff, or a Seed?
http://urbanext.illinois.edu/gpe/ case3/c3facts1.html
Learn about the parts of the seed, how they grow, and other ways plants reproduce.

INDEX

ABOUT THE AUTHOR

Jennifer Colby is a school librarian, and she also has a bachelor's degree in Landscape Architecture. By writing these books she has combined her talents for two of her favorite things. She likes to garden and grow her own food. In June she makes strawberry jam for her children to enjoy all year long.